LEAVING MY HOMELAND

After the Journey

My New Home After the
Democratic Republic of the
Congo

CRABTREE
PUBLISHING COMPANY
WWW.CRABTREEBOOKS.COM

Ellen Rodger

CRABTREE
PUBLISHING COMPANY
WWW.CRABTREEBOOKS.COM

Author: Ellen Rodger

Editors: Sarah Eason, Harriet McGregor, and Janine Deschenes

Proofreader and indexer: Wendy Scavuzzo

Editorial director: Kathy Middleton

Design: Paul Myerscough and Jessica Moon

Photo research: Rachel Blount

Production coordinator and Prepress technician: Ken Wright

Print coordinator: Katherine Berti

Consultant: Hawa Sabriye

Written, developed, and produced by Calcium

Publisher's Note: The story presented in this book is a fictional account based on extensive research of real-life accounts by refugees, with the aim of reflecting the true experience of refugee children and their families.

Photo Credits:
t=Top, c=Center, b=Bottom, l= Left, r=Right

Cover: Shutterstock

Inside: Jessica Moon: p. 29b; Shutterstock: pp. 5l, 8t; Arieliona: p. 24c; Arindambanerjee: pp. 22-23b; BalkansCat: pp. 14-15t; Brichuas: p. 18b; Chipmunk131: p. 1l; Curiosity: p. 15r; Sam Dcruz: p. 10t; EQRoy: p. 17t; Greatest Shots: p. 25t; Green 01: p. 26t; Greens87: p. 1bg; Hut Hanna: p. 24bl; Russ Heinl: p. 26c; IsoVector: p. 15t; Kirill Kalchenko: p. 12t; Helga Khorimarko: p. 19b; Cindy Lee: p. 23br; Lemberg Vector studio: p. 3; LineByLine: p. 6bl; Louisen: p. 19t; Michele Luppi: p. 10br; Adriana Mahdalova: p. 11cl; Mat277: p. 12-13c; Monkey Business Images: pp. 13b, 20-21b, 28b; Mspoint: pp. 17b, 28t; Olyvia: p. 18t; PamelaL: p. 7t; William Perugini: p. 18c; George Rudy: p. 21b; Cagkan Sayin: pp. 16-17b; Dayah Shaltes: p. 22t; John Simpson Photography: p. 27cr; SpeedKingz: p. 29r; Sudowoodo: pp. 11t, 23t, 29t; Alexandra Tyukavina: pp. 6-7c; VectorPlotnikoff: p. 20c; Alvaro Villanueva: p. 5r; WarmWorld: p. 24t; What's My Name: p. 10bl; Colin Woods: pp. 14-15b, 16t; Murat Irfan Yalcin: p. 5bl; © UNHCR: © UNHCR/Michelle Siu: p. 15c; Wikimedia Commons: Lisa Gansky: p. 27br; Julien Harneis: p. 9; MONUSCO: p. 8c; MONUSCO/Sylvain Liechti: p. 6br.

Library and Archives Canada Cataloguing in Publication

Title: My new home after the Democratic Republic of the Congo / Ellen Rodger.
Names: Rodger, Ellen, author.
Series: Leaving my homeland: after the journey.
Description: Series statement: Leaving my homeland: after the journey | Includes index.
Identifiers: Canadiana (print) 2019011469X | Canadiana (ebook) 20190114711 | ISBN 9780778764991 (softcover) | ISBN 9780778764878 (hardcover) | ISBN 9781427123732 (HTML)
Subjects: LCSH: Refugees—Congo (Democratic Republic)—Juvenile literature. | LCSH: Refugees—Canada—Juvenile literature. | LCSH: Refugee children—Congo (Democratic Republic)—Juvenile literature. | LCSH: Refugee children—Canada—Juvenile literature. | LCSH: Refugees—Social conditions—Juvenile literature. | LCSH: Congo (Democratic Republic)—History—1997—Juvenile literature. | LCSH: Congo (Democratic Republic)—Social conditions—Juvenile literature.
Classification: LCC HV640.5.A3 R63 2019 | DDC j305.23086/914096751—dc23

Library of Congress Cataloging-in-Publication Data

Names: Rodger, Ellen, author.
Title: My new home after the Democratic Republic of the Congo / Ellen Rodger.
Description: New York : Crabtree Publishing Company, [2019] | Series: Leaving my homeland: after the journey | Includes index.
Identifiers: LCCN 2019023017 (print) | LCCN 2019023018 (ebook) | ISBN 9780778764878 (hardcover) | ISBN 9780778764991 (paperback) | ISBN 9781427123732 (ebook)
Subjects: LCSH: Refugees--Congo (Democratic Republic)--Juvenile literature. | Refugees--Canada--Juvenile literature. | Refugee children--Congo (Democratic Republic)--Juvenile literature. | Refugee children--Canada--Juvenile literature.
Classification: LCC HV640.5.A3 R626 2019 (print) | LCC HV640.5.A3 (ebook) | DDC 362.7/791408996071--dc23
LC record available at https://lccn.loc.gov/2019023017
LC ebook record available at https://lccn.loc.gov/2019023018

Crabtree Publishing Company

www.crabtreebooks.com   1-800-387-7650

Printed in the U.S.A./082019/CG20190712

Published in Canada
Crabtree Publishing
616 Welland Ave.
St. Catharines, Ontario
L2M 5V6

Published in the United States
Crabtree Publishing
PMB 59051
350 Fifth Avenue, 59th Floor
New York, New York 10118

Published in the United Kingdom
Crabtree Publishing
Maritime House
Basin Road North, Hove
BN41 1WR

Published in Australia
Crabtree Publishing
Unit 3 – 5 Currumbin Court
Capalaba
QLD 4157

What Is in This Book?

Etienne's Story: From the DRC to Canada

Bonjour, hello! I am Etienne. I live in Montréal in Canada, but I did not always live here. I came to Canada with my mother and my sister, Martine, from the Democratic Republic of the Congo (DRC). We were **refugees***, forced to leave the DRC because it was not safe. There is a lot of war and violence in my* **homeland***.*

When I was eight years old, I was taken from my family by dangerous men. They forced me to be a soldier in a **militia***. Militias were fighting the government for control in my homeland. They forced children like me to fight and kill. It is against international law, but no one is able to stop them. One day, I escaped from the militia. I ran and ran, hoping they would not find me. Eventually, I was rescued and found my mother and sister.*

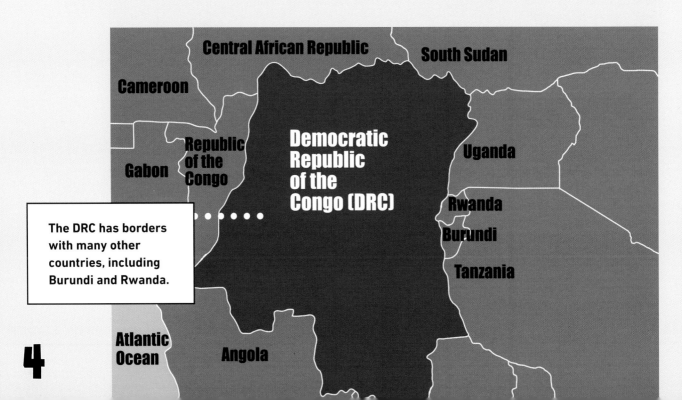

Central African Republic

South Sudan

Cameroon

Republic of the Congo

Gabon

Democratic Republic of the Congo (DRC)

Uganda

Rwanda

Burundi

Tanzania

The DRC has borders with many other countries, including Burundi and Rwanda.

Atlantic Ocean

Angola

4

UN Rights of the Child

Every child has **rights**, including the right to live with their parents, or family that cares for them. Think about these rights as you read this book.

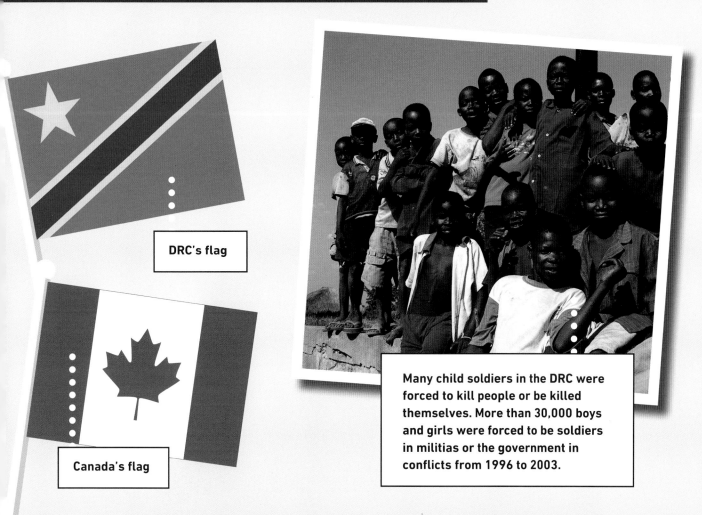

DRC's flag

Canada's flag

Many child soldiers in the DRC were forced to kill people or be killed themselves. More than 30,000 boys and girls were forced to be soldiers in militias or the government in conflicts from 1996 to 2003.

*We fled the DRC and went to a refugee camp in Burundi. At the camp, we were **registered** as refugees. My sister became very sick. The food was not good, and she almost died. But we were lucky. After three years, we were accepted to come to Canada and live with my aunt in Montréal. But we came without my father and my older brother, Claude. They are missing in the DRC. We still do not know if they are alive. My mother says she will never give up hope that we will find them one day.*

My Homeland, the DRC

The DRC is a country with an **unstable** recent history. It is located in Central Africa. The DRC is a land of lush forests, with beautiful lakes and rivers. It is also rich in **natural resources**. Other countries wanted to gain control of its people and the natural resources. So Belgium controlled the DRC from 1908 until 1960, when the country became **independent**.

The governments that ruled the DRC after independence were cruel and unfair. They wanted the country's wealth for themselves and their families. They often jailed or killed anyone who stood up to them. This made life in the DRC very difficult and dangerous.

The DRC is home to many different ethnic groups. **Fighting between these different groups has forced many people to leave their homes.**

The government of the DRC canceled elections that were meant to happen in 2016. It did this so it could remain in power longer.

Christians, who make up the majority of the population of the DRC, travel to Mount Mangengenge, near the capital city, Kinshasa, to pray for peace.

The most recent war, the Second Congo War, lasted five years (1998–2003). There is still ongoing violence that **displaces** people throughout the country. Some of the fighting is between different groups and the government. Some is ethnic, involving people from different tribal groups. Many Congolese people feel the violent struggles will never end.

Story in Numbers

As of February 2019, there are believed to be

826,820

refugees from the DRC in Africa; 38.4 percent are in Uganda, 10.3 percent in Tanzania, 9.8 percent in Rwanda, 9.3 percent in Burundi, and 7.3 percent in South Africa.

Etienne's Story: Leaving My Homeland

When I was a young boy, we lived in the city of Lubumbashi. We had a good life. My father was a teacher, but things got bad. My father spoke out against the government because he felt they were unfair to the people. My father was threatened by people who supported the government. To keep us safe, he sent me, my mother, and my sister away to my grandmother's farm. My father and Claude stayed in Lubumbashi.

The "blue helmets," or berets, are United Nations (UN) troops that have been sent to areas such as the DRC to keep the peace.

Canada

Montréal

North
Atlantic
Ocean

The journey from Burundi, where Etienne stayed in a refugee camp, to Montréal in Canada, is more than 7,030 miles (11,300 km).

DRC Burundi

I was in my grandmother's fields when militia soldiers came. They took me and some other boys from the village. They told us we must hurt people or we would be killed. I followed orders and did terrible things. Every day, I was scared. I thought that soon I would be like some of the older boys in the militia. They did not remember their families. They did not care about anything anymore. But I had luck with me, because I escaped and found some people who helped me. I was sent to a **reintegration** center that took in child soldiers like me. The center helped us and sent us to school.

These children live in Nyanzale. This is a camp in North Kivu province in the DRC for people who had to flee their homes.

The people at the center helped me find my mother and sister. I was scared they would not want me anymore. But my mother was not afraid of me. She said it would be unsafe to return to my grandmother's village, though. Many people there did not trust child soldiers. So we traveled to a refugee camp in Burundi. We registered as refugees. After three years in the camp, we were sent to Canada.

A New Life

It is not easy to leave your home, friends, and family. **Migrants**, **asylum seekers**, and refugees take great risks. They want a chance to build better and safer lives in a new place. In countries such as the DRC, people flee because their lives are in danger. Those who go to safer areas in their own country are called internally displaced persons (IDPs).

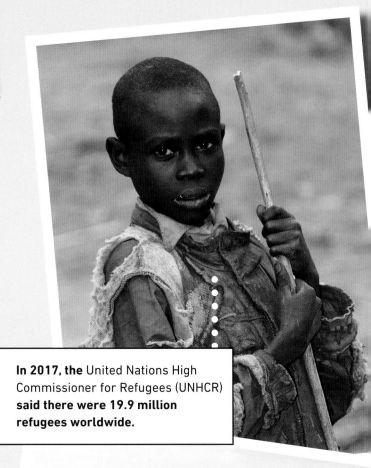

In 2017, the United Nations High Commissioner for Refugees (UNHCR) said there were 19.9 million refugees worldwide.

IDPs stay within their own country, but they are still **vulnerable**. They have little protection from violence. They may move many times. Some may later seek asylum in another country.

Many IDPs live in informal camps. These are camps set up outside of cities or villages. They have few or no services, including water.

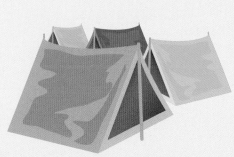

UN Rights of the Child

Governments have a responsibility to ensure people's rights are protected.

Some refugee camps offer refugees safety and schooling. This woman is learning dressmaking in a camp in Kenya.

Asylum seekers are people who travel to a new country and apply for protection there. Most often, they must stay in a crowded refugee camp until their application is reviewed. If they are approved, they can stay in the country as refugees. If their request is rejected, they are returned to their homeland.

When someone is registered as a refugee, it means they can be chosen for **resettlement** in another country. But millions of registered refugees never leave the refugee camps. Only a very small number of refugees worldwide are resettled in western countries, such as the United States or Canada.

Etienne's Story: Arriving in Canada

My first memory of Canada was the snow and cold. It was winter and the cold actually hurt my body. It was even hard to breathe, but I do not know if that was the freezing air or my fear and excitement about being in a strange land.

At first we lived with my aunt, Marie-Ange, and cousins, Imani and Fabrice. Then we got our own apartment close to them. I was at school in a class with children of my own age. But at the same time, I was older and younger than everyone. I was older because of my life experiences. I was younger because I had so much learning to catch up on.

Winter in Montréal is long and cold. On average, the temperature can drop down to 16 °F (-9 °C).

Bonjour! Etienne here! This is my first guest post here on Imani's blog! I am writing from Montréal. I go to a good school. My teacher is much less strict than teachers at home in the DRC. There are some other children like me—they came from other places in the world, too. Yesterday was Shrove Tuesday. We had pancakes at school. They are like a flat cake with sweet syrup that comes from a maple tree. Very delicious! Etienne

Marie-Ange came to Canada many years ago. My cousins do not know what it was like to live in the DRC. But I miss my family back home. Things are so different here. I am so different. Sometimes, I think I am not living the same life as my mother and sister. At school, I pay attention. Then I hear a noise such as a squeak of a chair and I freeze. Other times, anger bursts from me. I scare people, even though I do not mean to.

Concentrating on lessons in school can be very difficult for children who have suffered and seen violence during times of conflict.

Story in Numbers

In 2018, Canada had a total of

55,388

refugee claims. Of these, 14,790 were accepted. 162 were from the DRC.

A New Home

Most refugees are very **resilient**. This helps them adjust to life in a new place. Refugees must make huge changes to how they live. They may have to learn new languages and new skills for school or jobs.

In Canada, refugees are helped by the government and other groups. To help them start over, the government gives them money for up to a year, or until they can get jobs. When a refugee arrives in Canada, they are helped by the Resettlement Assistance Program for the first four to six weeks. This may include being picked up from the airport when they arrive, or being given a temporary place to live. The program also helps refugees find such things as schools, language classes, and health care.

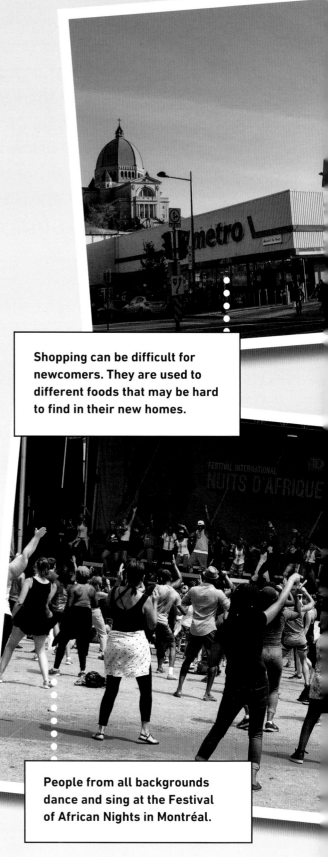

Shopping can be difficult for newcomers. They are used to different foods that may be hard to find in their new homes.

People from all backgrounds dance and sing at the Festival of African Nights in Montréal.

UN Rights of the Child

All children have the right to go to school and receive a good quality education.

This refugee from the DRC has found work in the kitchen of a hospital in Montréal. Refugees need to find work to support themselves and their families.

In addition, Québec has a refugee resettlement program. Refugees are given a hotel room for a few days after they arrive. They are then given help with things such as finding an apartment.

Privately **sponsored** refugees are supported by groups of five or more ordinary Canadians or community groups. These groups agree to support a refugee family for at least a year. The sponsors assist with finding housing, clothing, and schools. They may also help with other things, such as applying for jobs.

Etienne's Story: My New Home

My mother works with my aunt in her restaurant. It is an African restaurant with Congolese food. After school, I go there with Martine. We do our homework and play games at a table in the back. My aunt also gives me jobs to keep me busy. I cannot be "lazing around" near her!

Sometimes on weekends, Fabrice delivers food for my aunt. He takes me on deliveries. He plays a lot of cool music in the car. Fabrice goes to university. He is also a musician and knows a lot of people who play music. Some of them play on Saturday nights at the restaurant. Last week, there was a musician who played in a famous band in the DRC. I want to be like my favorite Congolese stars!

Montréal has many summer festivals of music and culture. This man prepares Spanish paella at an outdoor kiosk.

These musicians are playing African djembe and dundun drums at Montréal's Mont Royal Park.

Universities, such as this one in Montréal, include students from many backgrounds and cultures.

Last week, we heard from my mother's cousin, Laurent. He left the DRC before we did. He now lives in South Africa. He has been there for 20 years, but only has temporary permission to live there. Temporary means that it is not forever. Laurent says there are gangs of dangerous men who beat up asylum seekers in South Africa. Different ethnic groups are fighting each other there, too.

Laurent heard from my grandmother in the DRC. She said there was new violence near her village. But there was still no news of my father and brother. Laurent says we may never know what happened to them. My mother says we are lucky to be refugees in Canada. We will not be kicked out, and we have family and friends here to help us.

Story in Numbers

Between 2015 and 2017,

84,000

refugees were resettled in Canada. Almost half of them were children.

A New School

People from all over the world have settled in Canada. The government says that people from all backgrounds have a right to equal treatment and protection.

In Québec, public education is free for everyone. The children of refugees and immigrants attend French-language schools. No matter the language spoken at home, refugee children learn French, which is Québec's official language. This means refugee and immigrant children often speak two or three languages.

All children aged 6 to 16 must attend school in Québec, and boys and girls attend school together. After school, students look for work or apply to college. To attend university, they first spend two years at a college called a CEGEP.

Québec works to help different ethnic groups be understanding toward one another. For example, the government supports music and culture festivals that bring together people from different groups.

UN Rights of the Child

Children have the right to be who they are no matter where they live, what their parents do, what language they speak, or what their religion or culture is.

Many refugees rely on the support of family or friends already in the country. They also depend on churches and community centers for support and a sense of belonging.

Refugee children who come from areas of conflict, such as the DRC, may find their new school life challenging. They may be dealing with emotional difficulties, such as post-traumatic stress disorder (PTSD), after seeing violence in their homeland. Many refugee children must try to fit in and learn in an unfamiliar culture. Their teachers may not have the skills or resources to deal with cultural differences. They might also feel torn between the culture of their homeland and their new home. It can take time for refugee children to feel that they belong in a new country.

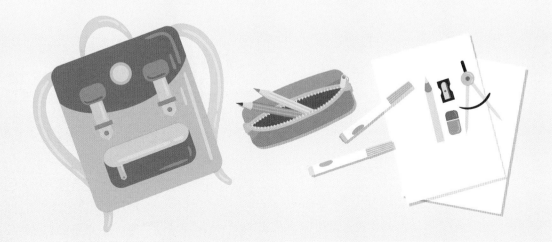

Etienne's Story: A New Way of Learning

A while ago, my teacher met with my mother. She told her that it is hard for me to make friends, and that I cannot always focus and do well in school. But I want to have friends, and I want to do well. I want to be educated like my father, and make my family proud of me.

My mother and I then met Madam Giroux. She is a school **psychologist**. She enrolled me in the **Big Brothers Big Sisters** program. I see her every Wednesday now. Sometimes, we read or play games. Other times, we talk. There are things I cannot tell people about being a child soldier. Madam Giroux says that is okay and that she believes in me. I think I am starting to believe that I can be a good person again.

Story in Numbers
20 to 30 percent
of refugees in Canada live in Québec.

I now have a Big Brother. His name is Luc. We meet every week and he is teaching me to play chess. We do other cool things, too. Last week was amazing because we went to a Montréal Impact soccer game. They are Montréal's pro soccer team. I also have a tutor who helps with my reading and writing. My math skills have improved a lot. Things are starting to work out.

Teachers and mentors can help refugee students adjust to a new culture and way of learning.

Hi Luc,
I wanted to e-mail to say thank you for all the help you have given me. I feel more confident because of our friendship. Playing chess with you has been great! My mother is really pleased that I am learning some new skills. She says maybe this summer I can start to play in a soccer league with other boys my age. Maybe you and I could try out some soccer skills when I see you next.
Thanks again,
Etienne

Chess is a game that helps develop focus and concentration skills.

Everything Changes

Countries such as Canada and the United States have signed international agreements. These agreements allow refugees to stay in the country permanently. Not everyone in these countries agrees with the agreements. Refugees are not always treated with kindness and respect. Some groups of people are hostile toward refugees. These people are a small group. However, their views can have an effect on others.

In 2017, 20,594 asylum seekers entered Canada **illegally**. They crossed the border in forests and farm fields. Most of these crossings were in Québec. Many of the asylum seekers were originally from Africa and Caribbean countries, but had been living in the United States. They were afraid of staying in the United States.

This is an official border crossing from the United States into Canada. Thousands of people cross between the two countries each day.

This welcome sign is held up during a rally to welcome refugees to Canada.

In the United States, more people have been speaking against refugees. Some are even violent toward them. In Canada, too, some people do not want refugees in the country. Groups there protest the migrants arriving near the border. Other groups want to show migrants that they are welcome. They often hold up signs to say that they welcome refugees into their country.

In 2019, the Canadian government said that it wants to stop people from entering the country illegally. It wants people to claim asylum only at official border crossings. But organizations that support refugees say that Canada should accept all asylum claims. They say that keeping people safe is the most important thing.

Etienne's Story: My New Way of Life

I have some news: I am learning to play the guitar! Madame Giroux got me into a music therapy program. Albert, my music **therapist**, is a musician who helps me with some problems. Madame Giroux has helped me learn about post-traumatic stress disorder (PTSD). I have it from my time as a child soldier. It makes me stressed and angry. "Music has the charms to soften rocks," Albert jokes. I am the rock. He makes me laugh.

At first, we just listened to music. Then we played instruments. I like the guitar best. Albert is helping me learn to play. Now we are writing songs. I feel like I can get my feelings out with music better than any other way.

Music therapy helps people improve their mental health and well-being.

UN Rights of the Child

Children have the right to choose their own friends and join or set up groups, as long as what they do is not harmful to others.

People in Montréal's Carifiesta Parade celebrate Caribbean culture and immigration. Immigration is the act of moving to live in a new country.

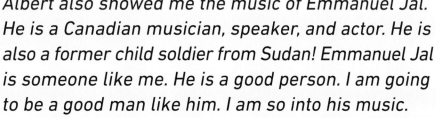

Albert also showed me the music of Emmanuel Jal. He is a Canadian musician, speaker, and actor. He is also a former child soldier from Sudan! Emmanuel Jal is someone like me. He is a good person. I am going to be a good man like him. I am so into his music.

My mother thought I was doing well in my studies and was helping at home and in the restaurant, so she decided I could play soccer, too. I cannot tell you how happy this makes me! Last week, my whole family and my Big Brother Luc came to see me play. I almost scored a goal, too!

Etienne's Story: Looking to the Future

Today was an exciting day—my aunt became a Canadian citizen. Marie-Ange has lived in Canada for many years. My cousins are Canadian citizens because they were born here. But my aunt never got her Canadian citizenship until now. She said having us here was her final push to become Canadian.

My aunt took a test on the history, government, and people of Canada. Later, we all went to a ceremony. She made a citizenship promise. We had a party at the restaurant after the ceremony. My mother says that in a few years, we can apply to become Canadian citizens. I am happy about this, but sad that my father and Claude are not here with us.

To pass the citizenship test, the subject must answer questions about Canada, including questions about its many cities, people, and their ways of life.

UN Rights of the Child

You have the right to an identity, which no one can take away from you.

Bonjour friends! I hope you read this and are well. This is my second post on Imani's blog. We are all well. Martine graduated from Grade 8, and I am continuing in high school. We all went to Orange Julep to celebrate. It is a restaurant in a big orange ball. Fabrice says this is where "all the cool cats are at." He is a big joker. I learn all my English from him. We are becoming real Montréalers. For my birthday, Fabrice, Martine, and Imani gave me a Montréal Canadiens jersey. They are a hockey team here. People are crazy for hockey here. Actually, I am starting to like hockey, too. Imagine that! But I still think soccer is a better sport. I play soccer at school. I wish you could see us. We miss you all. Etienne

Orange Julep is a well-known Montréal restaurant where people line up for creamy orange drinks.

The Montréal Canadiens are a National Hockey League (NHL) team. The team has fans all over the world.

Do Not Forget Our Stories!

A refugee's journey is long and difficult. Refugee children are especially vulnerable. They are at risk, even in their **host country**. They may have suffered during war and conflict. Some lose parents and other family members. If they are resettled, they may find themselves torn between two worlds. They may not feel at home in either.

Some children from the DRC were taken at a young age and were forced to be soldiers. If they escape, it can be difficult for them to adapt to normal life. Child soldiers also face **discrimination**. People fear them because of what they were forced to do. They may be years behind in school, and may suffer from PTSD. But they can learn and contribute to a better society.

Bake sales are one way volunteers can help raise money for refugee assistance.

UN Rights of the Child

Children have the right to equal opportunities in education and life.

Refugees are sometimes the targets of xenophobia. This is the fear and dislike that some people feel for people from other countries. Xenophobia and **racism** are wrong, and harmful for all. Refugees need help. If given a chance, they become good citizens. They work, own businesses, and pay **taxes** to the government. Their contributions make a country better.

Refugees get jobs, pay taxes, and eventually can earn as much as Canadians born in the country.

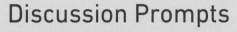

Discussion Prompts

1. Why is it important to be open-minded about refugees?
2. Think of some ways you can speak out against racism.
3. Why do some people fear former child soldiers?

Glossary

asylum seekers People looking for protection from a country

Big Brothers Big Sisters An organization that matches mentors with children who have similar interests

discrimination Unfair treatment of someone because of their race, religion, ethnic group, or other identifiers

displaces Forces from an area

ethnic groups Groups of people who have the same cultural or religious origin

homeland The country where someone was born or grew up

host country A country that offers to give refugees a home

illegally Not allowed by law

independent Free of outside control

mentors People who give someone else help or advice

migrants People who move from one place to another

militia A private army

natural resources Materials from nature that are useful

psychologist Someone who studies and treats the mind and behavior

racism The belief that people of some races are not equal to others

refugees People who flee from their own country to another due to unsafe conditions

registered Added to an official list

reintegration Rejoining society

resettlement To settle in a new or different place

resilient Able to recover from difficult situations

rights Privileges or freedoms protected by law

sponsored Has been given money or support to help improve their life

taxes Money paid to a government for services such as road maintenance

therapist Someone who treats psychological problems

United Nations High Commissioner for Refugees (UNHCR) A program that protects and supports refugees everywhere

unstable Often changing

vulnerable At risk of harm

Learning More

Books

Humphreys, Jessica Dee, and Michel Chikwanine. *Child Soldier: When Boys and Girls Are Used in War.* Kids Can Press, 2015.

Mancini, Candice. *Child Soldiers* (Global Viewpoints). Greenhaven Press, 2010.

Ruurs, Margriet. *Stepping Stones: A Refugee Family's Journey.* Orca Book Publishers, 2016.

Websites

www.amnesty.ca/blog/14-facts-about-refugees
Visit Amnesty International's website for facts about refugees in Canada.

www.childsoldiers.org
The website of an organization that is working to end the use of children as soldiers in conflict.

www.child-soldiers.org/who-are-child-soldiers
Find out more about child soldiers from Child Soldiers International, which helps schoolchildren learn about speaking out against injustice and the use of child soldiers.

www.unicef.org/rightsite/files/uncrcchilldfriendlylanguage.pdf
Read about the UN Convention on the Rights of the Child.

Index

About the Author

Ellen Rodger is a descendant of refugees who fled persecution and famine. She has written and edited many books for children and adults on subjects as varied as potatoes, social justice, war, and lice and fleas.